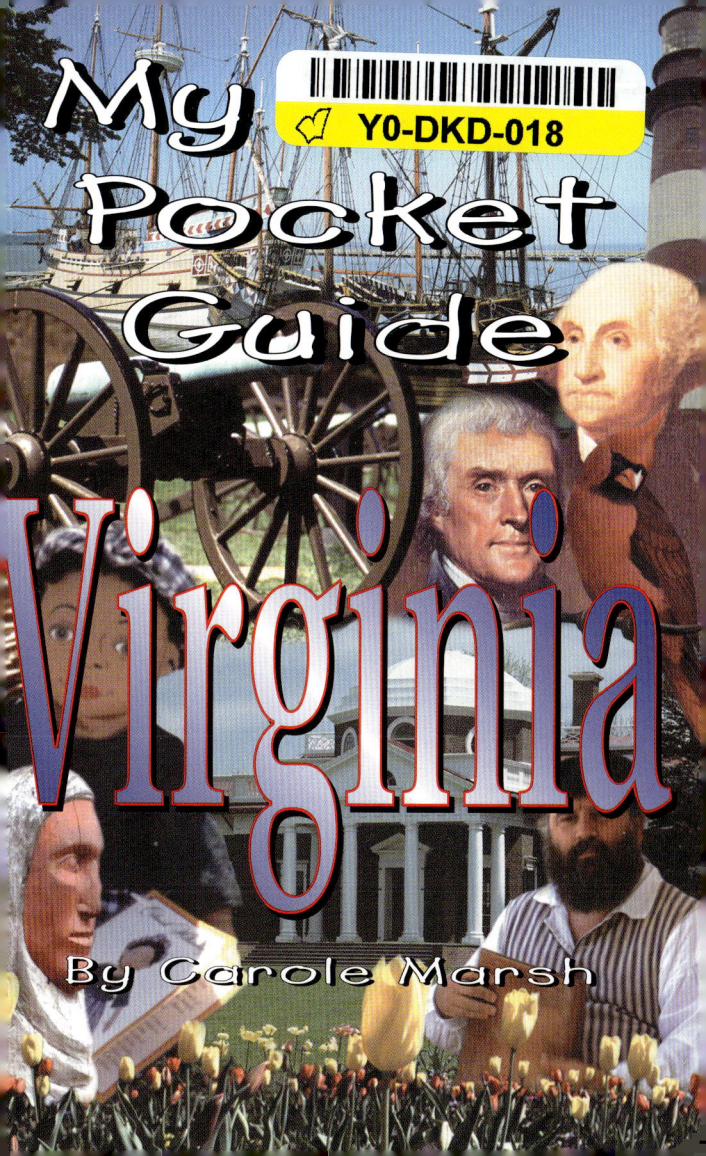

The Virginia Experience Team

Carole Marsh & Bob Longmeyer — Research/Writing
Michael Marsh — Website Design
Chad Beard — Production
Debra Sims — Customer Service
Sherry Moss & Sue Gentzke — Marketing
Michele Yother — President
Printed in the USA by **Print Craft, Inc.**
Brenda Crowley — Documentation & SOL Correlations
Danielle Omans — Editing
Steven Saint-Laurent, Marilyn Haas & Cecil Anderson — Graphic Design

Published by
GALLOPADE INTERNATIONAL
www.virginiaexperience.com
800-536-2GET
www.gallopade.com

ISBN 0793394562

©2000 Carole Marsh • First Edition • All Rights Reserved.
Character Illustrations by Lucyna A. M. Green.
No part of this publication may be reproduced in whole or in part, stored in a retrieval system, or transmitted in any form or by any means, electronic, mechanical, photocopying, recording or otherwise, without written permission from the publisher.

The Virginia Experience logo is a registered trademark of Carole Marsh and Gallopade International, Inc. A free catalog of The Virginia Experience Products is available by calling 800-536-2GET, or by visiting our website at www.virginiaexperience.com.

Gallopade is proud to be a member of these educational organizations and associations:

VAESP • VEMA • VIRGINIA COUNCIL FOR THE SOCIAL STUDIES • NSSEA • ASCD • SHOPA MEMBER (School, Home, & Office Products Association)

Other Virginia Experience Products
- The Virginia Experience!
- The BIG Virginia Reproducible Activity Book
- The Very Virginia Coloring Book
- My First Book About Virginia!
- Virginia "Jography": A Fun Run Through Our State
- Virginia Jeopardy!: Answers and Questions About Our State
- The Virginia Experience! Sticker Pack
- The Virginia Experience! Poster/Map
- Discover Virginia CD-ROM
- Virginia "Geo" Bingo Game
- Virginia "Histo" Bingo Game

A Word From the Author... (okay, a few words)...

Hi!

Here's your own handy pocket guide about the great state of Virginia! It really will fit in a pocket—I tested it. And it really will be useful when you want to know a fact you forgot, to bone up for a test, or when your teacher says, "I wonder . . ." and you have the answer—instantly! Wow, I'm impressed!

Get smart, have fun!

Carole Marsh

Virginia Basics explores your state's symbols and their special meanings!

Virginia Geography digs up the what's where in your state!

Virginia History is like traveling through time to some of your state's great moments!

Virginia People introduces you to famous personalities and your next-door neighbors!

Virginia Places shows you where you might enjoy your next family vacation!

Virginia Nature - no preservatives here, just what Mother Nature gave to Virginia!

All the real fun stuff that we just HAD to save for its own section!

- Virginia Basics
- Virginia Geography
- Virginia History
- Virginia People
- Virginia Places
- Virginia Nature
- Virginia Miscellany

State Name

Who Named You?

Virginia's official state name is...

The Commonwealth of Virginia

State Name

Word Definition

COMMONWEALTH: a nation or state governed by the people; from the word "commonweal," meaning "for the public good."

Statehood: June 25, 1788

Virginia was the 10th state to ratify the U.S. Constitution.

Virginia is one of the states to be on a year-2000 commemorative quarter! Look for it in cash registers everywhere!

State Name Origin

A Name of Royal Proportions!

Virginia was named for Queen Elizabeth I of England (reigned from 1558 until her death in 1603). An unmarried woman, she was nicknamed the "virgin queen." And that's how we get Virginia. (Get it?)

State Name Origin

The first English child born in North America, on August 18, 1587, on Roanoke Island, was named Virginia Dare!

State Nicknames

What's In A Name?

"The Commonwealth of Virginia" is not the only name by which Virginia is recognized. Like many other states, Virginia has several nicknames, official or unofficial!

State Nicknames

Old Dominion

Mother of Presidents

Mother of States

The Cavalier State

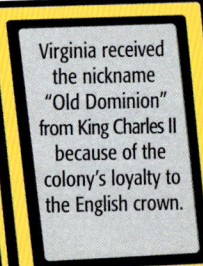

Mother of Statesmen

Virginia received the nickname "Old Dominion" from King Charles II because of the colony's loyalty to the English crown.

State Capital/Capitol

State Capital:
Richmond

Established 1742
Capital of Virginia since 1780

State Capitol

State Capital & Capitol

The capitol in Richmond is the second-oldest working capitol in the USA (after Maryland's).

Word Definition

CAPITAL: a town or city that is the official seat of government
CAPITOL: the building in which the government officials meet

State Government

Who's in Charge Here?

Virginia's GOVERNMENT has three branches:

- LEGISLATIVE
- EXECUTIVE
- JUDICIAL

State Government

The legislative branch is called the General Assembly.

LEGISLATIVE — TWO HOUSES: the Senate (40 members); House of Delegates (100 members)

EXECUTIVE — A governor, lieutenant governor, and attorney general

JUDICIAL — SUPREME COURT a chief justice plus six other justices

When you are 18 and register according to state laws — you can vote! So please do! Your vote counts!

The number of legislators and executors is determined by population, which is counted in the census every ten years; the numbers above are certain to change as Virginia grows and prospers!

State Flag

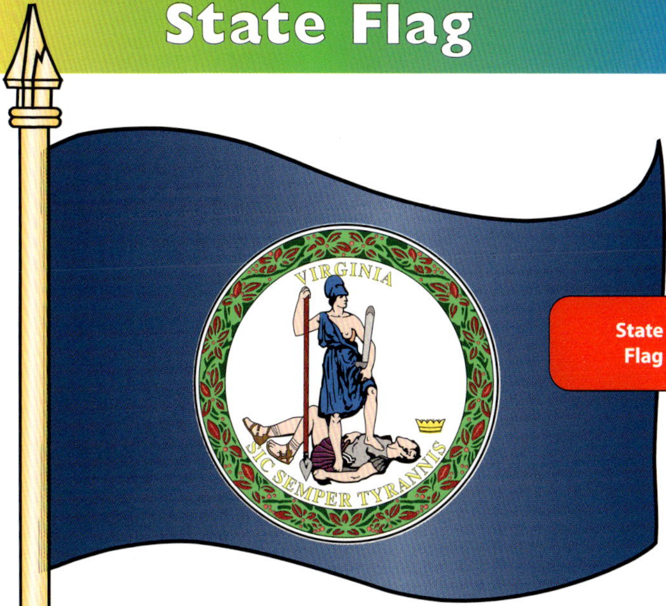
VIRGINIA
SIC SEMPER TYRANNIS

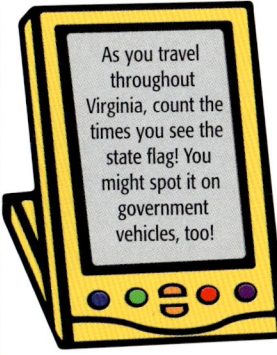

As you travel throughout Virginia, count the times you see the state flag! You might spot it on government vehicles, too!

The State Flag of Virginia was adopted in 1861. It is always found atop the state capitol, and all state, city and town buildings.

State Seal & Motto

State Seal

The Goddess of Virtue standing on the defeated body of Tyranny.

TYRANNY: power used in a cruel, oppressive manner

State Motto

Sic Semper Tyrannis

Virginia's state seal was designed by George Wythe, a signer of the Declaration of Independence.

That's Latin. It means, "Thus always to tyrants." (That means, "Take that, you big bully!")

State Bird

Birds of Red Feathers

The state bird of Virginia is the Northern Cardinal, *Cardinalis cardinalis,* known for its bright plumage and cheerful song.

State Bird

In 16th Century England, the cardinal was called "the Virginia Nightingale," for its beautiful melodies!

State Tree

FLOWERING DOGWOOD

The state tree of Virginia blooms in early spring. Its blossom is a tiny cluster of flowers surrounded by four white leaves that look like petals.

State Flower

Dogwood

The state flower of Virginia comes right from the state tree!

Dogwood - *Cornus florida*

State Flower

The actual flowers of the dogwood are the yellow clusters in the center of the white *bracts* (leaves).

The wood of the dogwood tree is so hard that it is often used for furniture. The bark yields a pigment used for black ink!

13

State Animal

American Foxhound

George Washington imported English foxhounds into Virginia for hunting. All American foxhounds are descended from these dogs!

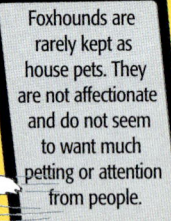

Foxhounds are rarely kept as house pets. They are not affectionate and do not seem to want much petting or attention from people.

RIDDLE: If the state flower got mixed up with the state dog, what would you have?

Answer: A Hound Dog... or a Foxwood?

State Shell & Fossil

"'T' was a brave man that first ate an OYSTER."

—*Crassotraea virginica*—

The state shell is the home of the oyster, which lives on the sea floor or on rocks in shallow water.

State Shell & Fossil

☐ ***To Do List:*** Measure your forearm from wrist to elbow — this is how big a full-grown oyster can be!

"'T' was a brave man that found this FOSSIL."

The ***Chesapecten jeffersonius*** was named in honor of Thomas Jefferson's interest in natural history, and it celebrates Chesapeake Bay, the largest estuary in the world!

The *Chesapecten jeffersonius* is the earliest described fossil found in North America. It lived millions of years ago, when wooly mammoths roamed the earth!

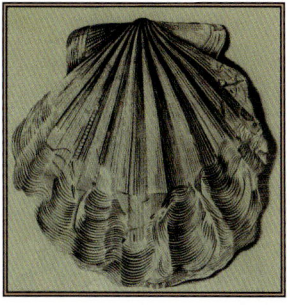

15

State Beverage

Milk is a nourishing drink that is also the source of butter, cheese, yogurt, and ice cream!

State Beverage

Moooo!

The first dairy cattle in what is now the United States were brought to the Jamestown colony in Virginia in 1611.

Virginia Milkshake

Take 2 scoops of vanilla ice cream, 1 cup of milk, and blend in a blender with 2 tablespoons peanut butter!

State Shape

A State in Good Shape

Virginia is shaped mostly like a triangle. A part of Virginia, the <u>Eastern Shore</u>, is not connected to the mainland!

State Shape

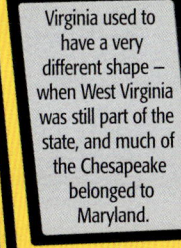

Virginia used to have a very different shape – when West Virginia was still part of the state, and much of the Chesapeake belonged to Maryland.

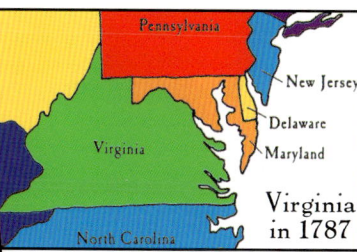

Virginia in 1787

21

State Location

Virginia is located on America's Eastern Seaboard. Its major cities are part of a megalopolis which stretches from Boston to Richmond.

State Location

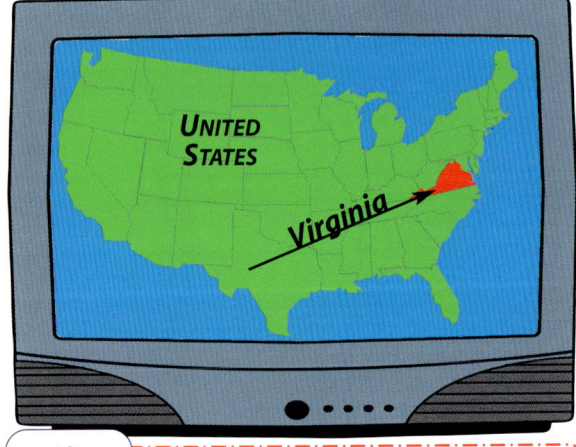

Word Definition

MEGALOPOLIS: A region made up of several large cities and their surrounding areas, together forming a single urban complex.

Virginia's Neighbors

On The Border!

These border Virginia:

States: North Carolina, Tennessee, Kentucky, West Virginia, Maryland

Bodies of water: Chesapeake Bay, Atlantic Ocean, Potomac River

Washington, D.C., the nation's capital, is also Virginia's neighbor!

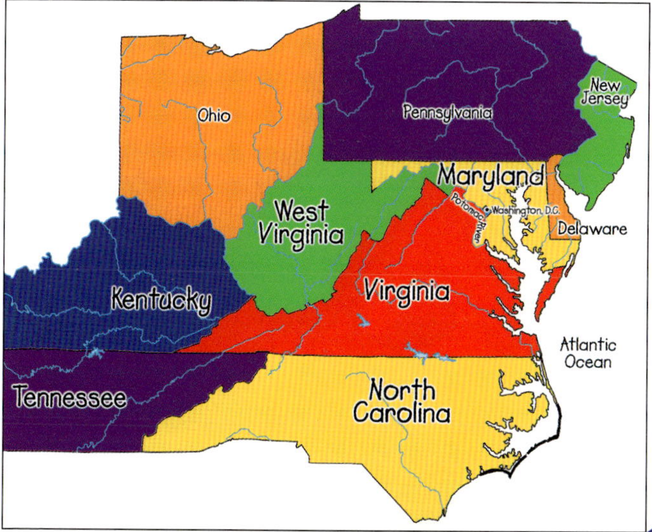

Virginia's Neighbors

23

East-West, North-South, Area

Virginia is 470 miles (756 kilometers) east to west... or west to east. Either way, it's a long drive!

Total Area: Approx. 42,326 square miles
Land Area: Approx. 39,598 square miles

Virginia is 200 miles (322 km) north to south... or south to north. Either way, it's still a long drive!

East–West
North–South
Area

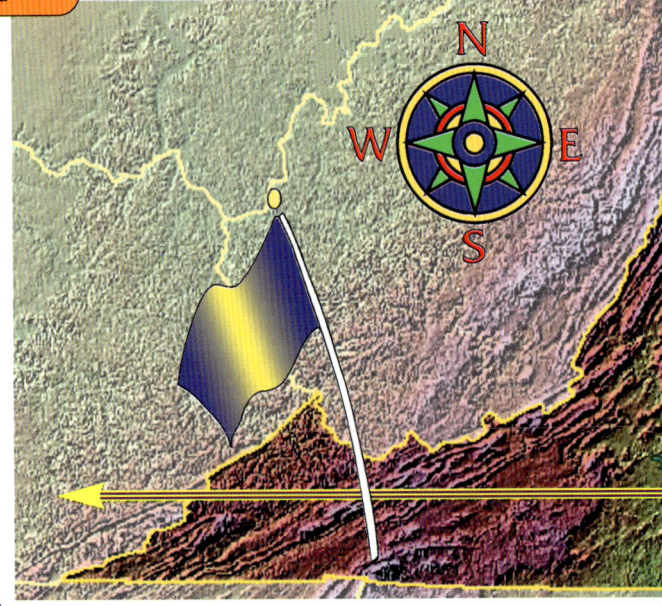

Highest & Lowest Points

Highest Point
Mount Rogers — 5,729 feet above sea level (1.09 miles; 1,746 meters)

Lowest Point
Sea Level — Along Virginia's extensive coastline.

"Whitetop" is the second highest mountain in Virginia, at 5,540 ft. It's more popular than Mt. Rogers because there's a better view from its peak!

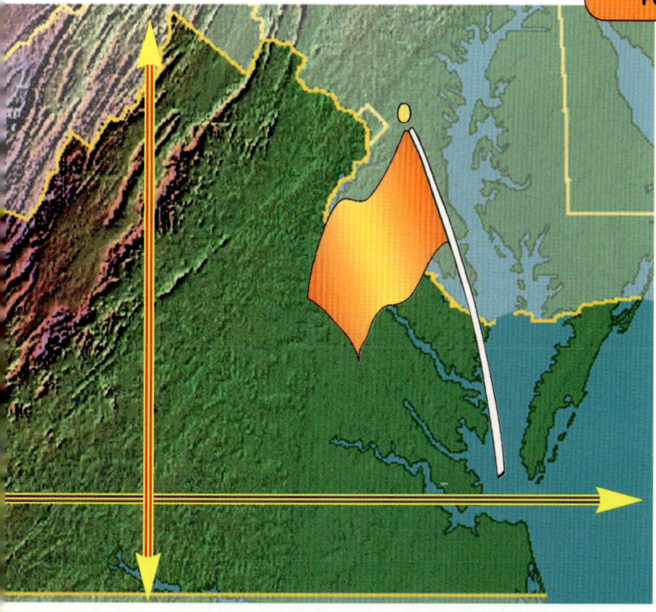

Highest & Lowest Points

Virginia Counties

I'm Countying on You!

Virginia is divided into 95 counties.

Word Definition

COUNTY: an administrative subdivision of a state or territory

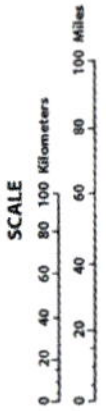

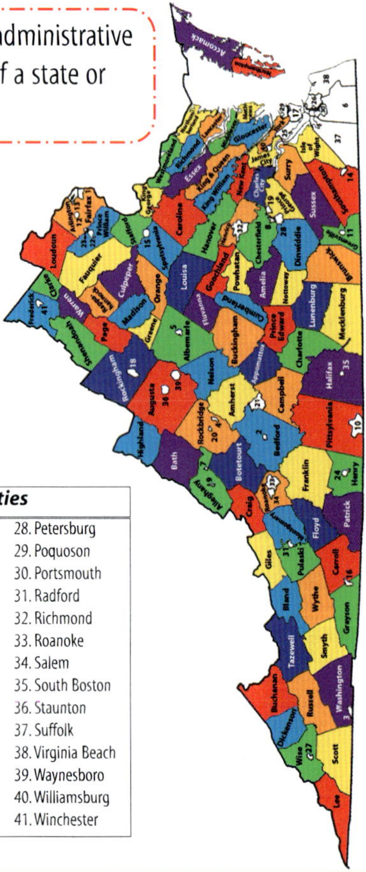

Virginia Counties

Independent Cities

1. Alexandria	14. Franklin	28. Petersburg
2. Bedford	15. Fredericksburg	29. Poquoson
3. Bristol	16. Galax	30. Portsmouth
4. Buena Vista	17. Hampton	31. Radford
5. Charlottesville	18. Harrisonburg	32. Richmond
6. Chesapeake	19. Hopewell	33. Roanoke
7. Clifton Forge	20. Lexington	34. Salem
8. Colonial Heights	21. Lynchburg	35. South Boston
9. Covington	22. Manassas	36. Staunton
10. Danville	23. Manassas Park	37. Suffolk
11. Emporia	24. Martinsville	38. Virginia Beach
12. Fairfax	25. Newport News	39. Waynesboro
13. Falls Church	26. Norfolk	40. Williamsburg
	27. Norton	41. Winchester

Natural Resources

Word Definition: NATURAL RESOURCES: things that exist in or are formed by nature

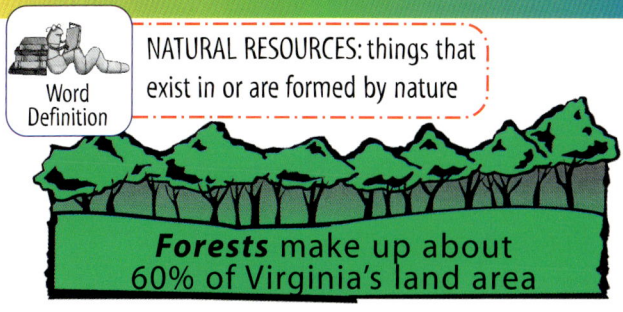

Forests make up about 60% of Virginia's land area

Minerals:
- Coal
- Kyanite
- Quartzite
- Soapstone
- Limestone
- Sandstone
- Sand and Gravel

Natural Resources

Deep-water ports allow large ships to deliver and export goods around the world.

Kyanite is used as an insulator because it is heat resistant. Some ovens used to manufacture glass and ceramics are lined with kyanite. Transparent kyanite is cut into gemstones for jewelry.

Weather

Weather, Or Not?!

Virginia's climate is generally mild and humid. The western mountains are usually cooler than the eastern coastal plain. Virginia has four distinct seasons, generous rainfall, and some snow.

Weather

Highest temperature: 110°F (43°C), Columbia, July 5, 1900 and Balcony Falls, July 15, 1954

°F=Degrees Fahrenheit °C=Degrees Celsius

Lowest temperature: -30°F (-34°C), Mountain Lake Bio Station, January 22, 1985

~ In 1853, Norfolk newspapers reported that catfish fell from the sky during a hailstorm.
~ In 1856, two snowstorms covered Lynchburg with 58 inches of snow.

Topography

Virginia's topography includes three land areas:
EAST: Atlantic Coastal Plain (Tidewater)
CENTRAL: Piedmont Plateau
WEST: Mountains, Ridges, and Valleys

FALL LINE: Runs from north to south and marks where rivers plunge downward on their trip to the sea!

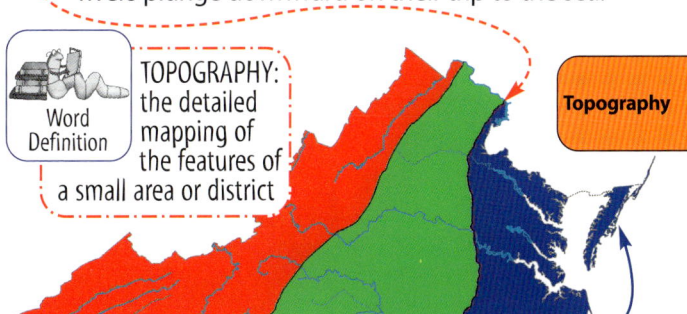

Word Definition — TOPOGRAPHY: the detailed mapping of the features of a small area or district

Topography

The Allegheny (Appalachian) Plateau in southwestern Virginia is the location of many coal deposits.

Delmarva Peninsula: The southernmost part of this peninsula is the part of Virginia separated from the rest of the state by the Chesapeake Bay. Maryland and Delaware are also a part of this peninsula...

DELMARVA
DELaware
MARyland
Virgini**A**

—*get it?*

29

Mountain Ranges & Peaks

Mountains
1. White Top Mountain
2. Massanutten Mountain
3. Brushy Mountain
4. Walker Mountain
5. Clinch Mountain

Ranges
Allegheny
Appalachian
Blue Ridge
Shenandoah

Virginia Geography

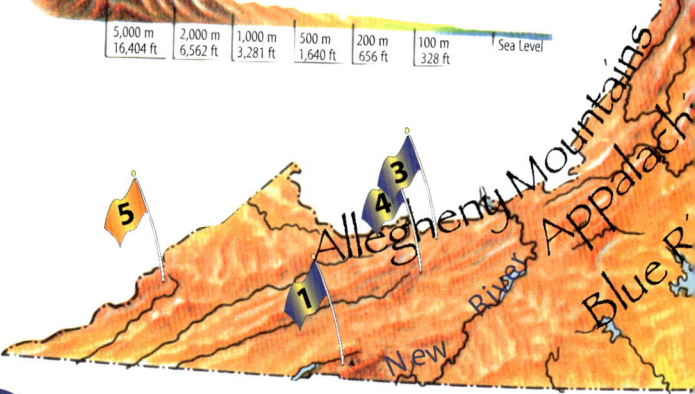

30

Major Rivers

The longest river wholly within Virginia is the James River. The Potomac River forms most of Virginia's northern boundary.

Potomac
Rappahannock
York
James
Roanoke
New

Major Rivers

31

Major Lakes & Reservoirs

John H. Kerr Reservoir
Claytor Lake
John W. Flannagan Reservoir

Lake Anna
Lake Gaston
Leesville Reservoir
Philpott Reservoir
Smith Mountain Lake
South Holston Lake

Major Lakes & Reservoirs

Lake Drummond, in the Dismal Swamp, is Virginia's largest natural lake, covering 3,200 acres. It may have been made by a meteor!

Word Definition — RESERVOIR: a body of water stored for public use

Cities & Towns

Have you heard these wonderful Virginia city, town, and crossroad names? Perhaps you can start your own collection! (Place names appear in COLOR.)

I wonder if there was a BIRDSNEST on the ARK? If the BISHOP falls down, that's just the BREAKS! On payday, I can get CASH or CHECK. While I swim with the DOLPHIN in the sea, I can watch the ECLIPSE in the sky! I always order FRIES. HENRY got HURT and lost his INDEPENDENCE for awhile. Check the INDEX; it's pretty LIVELY! I'd walk MILES to find a MINERAL. It's hard to be a braggart in MODEST TOWN. I have NEW HOPE that I'll strike it rich in OILVILLE! It was a brave man who first ate an OYSTER! A PILOT flew into a RADIANT sunset which had a great SUPPLY of TIPTOP clouds, some even in TRIANGLE shape! Did UNO I was a WISE person? Don't get caught in a WOLF TRAP!

Cities & Towns

33

Transportation

Major Interstate Highways
I-64, I-66, I-77, I-81, I-85, I-95

The Chesapeake Bay Bridge-Tunnel connects the mainland with the Eastern Shore.

Transportation

Railroads

In the early 1990s, Virginia had 3,286 miles (5,288 km) of railroad track and is served by Amtrak, Conrail, CSX Transportation, and Norfolk Southern Corp.

Major Airports
Dulles International
Washington National
Norfolk International
Richmond International

Seaports
Hampton Roads
Newport News
Norfolk
Portsmouth
Chesapeake

Timeline

1607	Jamestown settlement established
1624	Virginia a royal British colony
1676	Bacon's Rebellion
1699	Williamsburg named capital
1775	Revolutionary War begins
1776	Declaration of Independence signed
1788	Virginia becomes 10th state
1831	Nat Turner's Rebellion
1861	Virginia secedes from Union; Civil War begins
1865	Civil War ends
1870	Virginia rejoins Union
1920	Women get vote
1941	Virginians serve in World War II
1964	Civil Rights Act passed
1988	Virginia celebrates bicentennial
1999	Virginians on Internet
2001	Virginia enters 21st century!

Virginia History Timeline

Between June 1 and June 3, 1864, at the Battle of Cold Harbor, 7,000 Union soldiers were felled in one 20-minute period.

Early History

Here come the humans!

Early History

As early as 9500 B.C., Paleo (ancient) people lived in Virginia. They may have originally come across a frozen bridge of land between Asia and today's Alaska. If so, they slowly traveled south and east until some settled in what would one day become the state of Virginia.

These early people were nomadic hunters who traveled in small bands. They camped when seasons offered hunting, fishing, and fruit and nut gathering.

36

Early Indians

Native Americans Once Ruled!

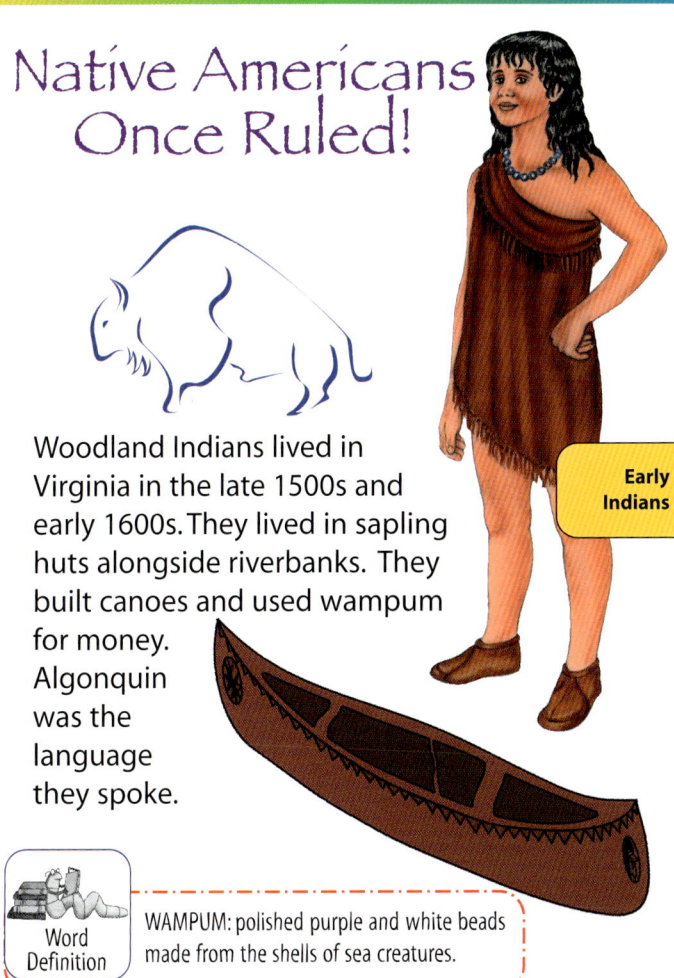

Woodland Indians lived in Virginia in the late 1500s and early 1600s. They lived in sapling huts alongside riverbanks. They built canoes and used wampum for money. Algonquin was the language they spoke.

Early Indians

Word Definition
WAMPUM: polished purple and white beads made from the shells of sea creatures.

Exploration

Land Ho!

Early explorers to Virginia found travel difficult because of thick forests and a lack of accurate maps. They returned to Spain and England with tales of a "paradise." Often, they forgot to add that there would be great hardships in taming the land, which was already occupied with native people!

Early Explorers

Explorers, missionaries, and adventurers came from Europe on ships in the 1500s.

38

Colonization

Home, Sweet, Home

In 1606, King James I granted a land charter to the Virginia Company of London. The colonists were supposed to explore the area, build a fort, prepare for a larger settlement, and convert the Indians to Christianity. They also were ordered to find a way to make money to pay for their venture!

Virginia Colonies

In 1607, 105 colonists and 39 sailors sailed from England on the Susan Constant, Godspeed, and Discovery. It took five months to reach Virginia. They named the place on the James River where they landed Jamestown, after their king, James I.

Jamestown was plagued by mosquitoes and wooden buildings that were always burning down!

Jamestown was the capital of the Virginia Colony for almost 100 years!

Tobacco

The Sot Weed!

This was the crop that the colonists finally learned would make money for them. The dried or "cured" leaves were shipped back to England, where they were used by the upper class people. In the colony, tobacco was used as money, even to pay for mail order brides!

Key Crop/Product

Tobacco was called the sot weed and many other ugly names by those who thought smoking and snuff were bad habits!

Early Capital

Welcome To Williamsburg!

In 1699, Williamsburg was made the new capital of the Virginia Colony. The people who lived there modeled the town after the great cities in Europe.

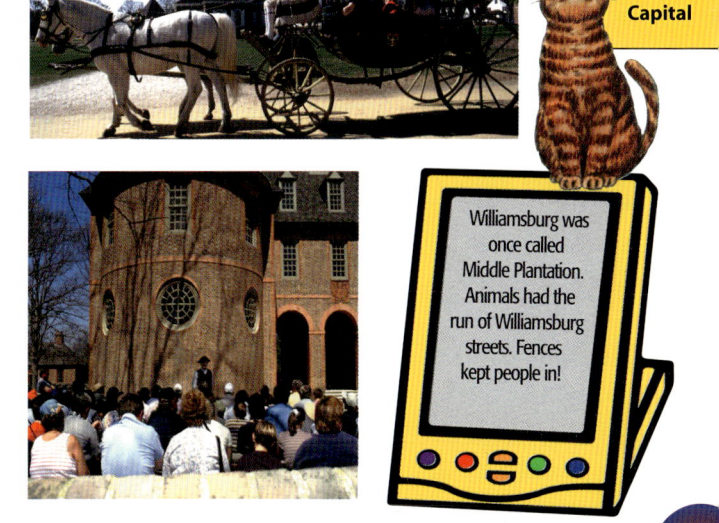

Early Capital

Williamsburg was once called Middle Plantation. Animals had the run of Williamsburg streets. Fences kept people in!

Slaves and Slavery

Of Human Bondage

Early in Virginia's history, blacks were brought from Africa to America to serve as slaves on plantations. While not all farmers owned slaves, some plantation owners could only enlarge their farms with slave labor. Over time, slaves rebelled. A slave named Gabriel led an uprising. Another slave named Nat Turner did the same thing. Abolitionists were against slavery. Some people helped blacks escape slavery on the Underground Railroad, a route to the northern states where they could live free.

The issue of slavery and states' rights led to the Civil War. In 1863, the Emancipation Proclamation freed the slaves.

Revolution

Freedom!

After the Virginia colony was established for awhile, some colonists felt that the royal governors ignored their ideas and concerns. In 1676, Nathaniel Bacon led a revolt against Governor William Berkeley. As time went by, more and more colonists wanted to be independent from British rule. In 1775, the colonies went to war with England. On July 4, 1776, the Declaration of Independence was signed.

Revolution

The Revolutionary War ended at Yorktown, Virginia after five long years. The British surrendered and the United States was born!

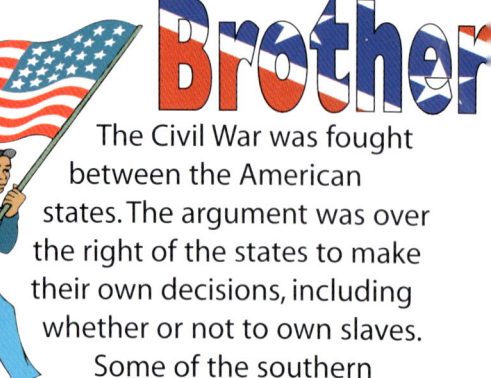

The Civil War!

Brother

The Civil War was fought between the American states. The argument was over the right of the states to make their own decisions, including whether or not to own slaves. Some of the southern states began to secede (leave) the Union. They formed the Confederate States of America. In 1861, Virginia joined this group. Richmond was named the capital.

The Civil War!

Word Definition — RECONSTRUCTION: the recovery and rebuilding period following the Civil War.

The Civil War!

vs. Brother

Many Civil War battles were fought in Virginia. Soldiers often found themselves fighting their former friends and neighbors, even relatives. After four long years, the Confederacy surrendered at Appomattox Court House.

The Civil War!

More people were killed during the Civil War than during World Wars I and II!

Famous Documents

Get It In Writing!

Famous Documents

The Charters of the Virginia Company of London

The Virginia Declaration of Rights

Declaration of Independence, 1776, written by Thomas Jefferson

The Virginia Statute for Religious Freedom, 1786

U.S. Constitution, 1787, Virginia's James Madison writes and argues for it! The Constitution went into effect in 1790.

The Monroe Doctrine

Immigrants

WELCOME TO AMERICA!

Virginians have come to the state from other states and many other countries on almost every continent! As time has gone by, Virginia's population has grown more diverse. This means that people of different races and from different cultures and ethnic backgrounds have moved to the state.

Virginia Immigrants

In the past, many immigrants came to Virginia from England, France, Germany, Scotland, Ireland, Hungary, and other European countries. Slaves migrated (involuntarily) from Africa. More recently, people have migrated to Virginia from South American and Asian countries. Only a certain number of immigrants are allowed to move to America each year. Many of these immigrants eventually become U.S. citizens.

47

Disasters & Catastrophes!

1900
Yellow Fever epidemic, Hampton

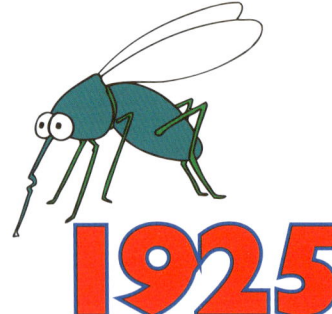

1925
October 2: The Church Hill Tunnel in Richmond collapsed, burying a locomotive and its ten freight cars - which are still buried today!

Virginia Disasters

1969
Hurricane Camille

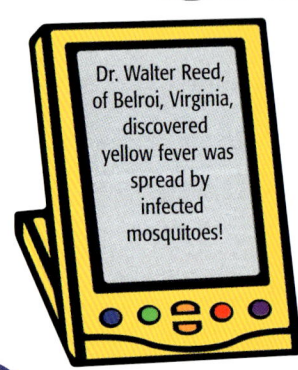

Dr. Walter Reed, of Belroi, Virginia, discovered yellow fever was spread by infected mosquitoes!

Legal Stuff

1882 Poll tax abolished

1908 Virginia Child Labor Law passed

1959 Virginia Supreme Court of Appeals outlaws school closing; integration of schools begins

Legal Stuff

1964 The Civil Rights Act of 1964 is passed

Women

1909
Virginia Equal Suffrage League formed

1918
First women admitted to a state college (William and Mary)

Virginia Women

1920
Women gain suffrage nationally through the 19th Amendment

1921
Two women elected to the Virginia General Assembly

1952
The Virginia General Assembly *finally* ratifies the 19th Amendment

Word Definition

SUFFRAGE: the right or privilege of voting

Wars

Fight!, Fight!, Fight!

Wars that Virginians participated in:
- **French and Indian War**
- **Revolutionary War**
- **Mexican War**
- **Civil War**
- **Spanish-American War**
- **World War I**
- **World War II**
- **Korean War**
- **Vietnam War**
- **Persian Gulf War**

Wars

Claim to Fame

Mother of Presidents

These presidents were born in Virginia:

George Washington
1st

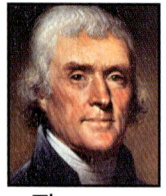

Thomas Jefferson
3rd

James Madison
4th

James Monroe
5th

William Henry Harrison
9th

John Tyler
10th

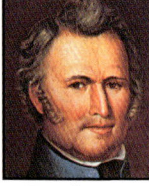

Zachary Taylor
12th

Woodrow Wilson
28th

Indian Tribes

- Pamunkey
- Mattaponi
- Monacan
- Potomac
- Cherokee
- Chickahominy
- Rappahannock
- Nansemond

Virginia's Indians spoke either the Algonquian, Siouan, or Iroquoian language.

Indian Tribes

The Pamunkey and Mattaponi still live on reservations in King William County. They honor treaties by paying $1.00 a year (or game and fish) in tax to Virginia's governor!

Two of Virginia's most famous Indians were Chief Powhatan and his daughter Pocahontas, friends of the early colonists!

Explorers and Settlers

Here, There, Everywhere!

CAPTAIN JOHN SMITH, English explorer and a president of the Jamestown Colony

RICHARD E. BYRD, one of first people to fly to the North Pole

Explorers & Settlers

WILLIAM CLARK and MERIWETHER LEWIS, explored the Louisiana Territory

MATTHEW MAURY, wrote the first textbook on modern oceanography; circumnavigated the world from 1826-30!

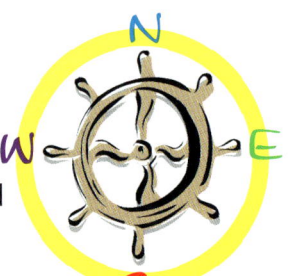

Virginia Founders

Founding Fathers

These Virginians played especially important roles in the creation of the United States of America!

GEORGE WASHINGTON — America's 1st president

THOMAS JEFFERSON — Wrote the Declaration of Independence

JAMES MADISON, born in Port Conway — Father of the Constitution

JAMES MONROE — Author of the Monroe Doctrine

PATRICK HENRY — Helped add the Bill of Rights to the U.S. Constitution

Brothers FRANCIS LIGHTFOOT and RICHARD HENRY LEE — Signers of the Declaration of Independence

GEORGE ROGERS CLARK — Revolutionary War soldier

GEORGE MASON — wrote the Virginia Declaration of Rights, the basis for the U.S. Bill of Rights

Founding Mothers

MARY DRAPER INGLES — Pioneer woman who escaped from Indians

MARTHA WASHINGTON — Wife of President George Washington

MISS COOKE — Started Richmond school for black children

ANNA WHITEHEAD BODEKER and ORRA GRAY LANGHORNE — Helped Virginia women get the right to vote

SARAH LEE FAIN and HELEN TIMMONS HENDERSON — First Virginia women elected to the House of Delegates

Virginia Founders

In 1619, the first women arrived in Virginia at the Jamestown colony. The ninety women were "mail order brides" for whom the settlers who married them paid 120 pounds of tobacco each for their ship's passage.

Famous African-Americans

SAMUEL CHAPMAN ARMSTRONG, founder, Hampton Normal and Industrial Institute

BOOKER T. WASHINGTON, slave who later founded the Tuskegee Institute, a school for black students in Alabama

SARAH GARLAND JONES, first African-American and woman to be certified by the Virginia State Board of Medicine

Famous African-Americans

ARTHUR ASHE, professional tennis player from Richmond, won 1975 Wimbledon

MAGGIE WALKER, first woman bank president in the U.S.

CARTER G. WOODSON, founded Negro History Week (now Black History Month)

Pirates and Ghosts

BLACKBEARD was called the "fiercest pirate of them all"! His real name may have been Ned Teach, Ed Thatch, or something similar. The pirate often visited Virginia's shores. After he was caught, his head was hung on a pole beside the Hampton River, now called Blackbeard's Point. Is his treasure buried somewhere in the Tidewater?

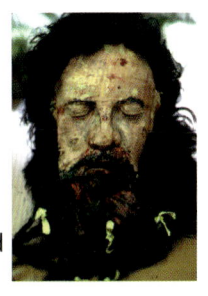

DID SOMEONE SAY BOO!?

Ghosts of the Refusal Room at Carter's Grove
The Insolent Hostess of Castle Hill
Dr. Blair, Sarah, and the Curse Tree
The "Gray Lady" of Hawes House
The West Point Light Ghost
Evelyn Byrd of Westover
The Woman in Black
The Room 403 Ghost
Lady Ann Skipwith
Chief Black Foot
Mad Ann Bailey
Old Crump
Belle Boyd

Pirates & Ghosts

Blackbeard swore only he and the Devil knew the whereabouts of his treasure, and the one who lived the longest could have it all!

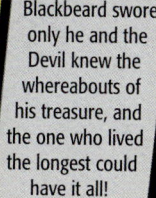

Sports Figures

ARTHUR ASHE, first African-American to win Wimbledon men's tennis title

SAM SNEAD, won more than 100 professional golf tournaments!

EPPA RIXEY, first Virginian elected to the Baseball Hall of Fame (1936)

Sports Figures

SECRETARIAT, to some the greatest race horse that ever lived

MARY MEAGHER PLANT, two-time Olympic gold medalist in swimming

Entertainers

- ★ **PEARL BAILEY**, singer
- ★ **ELLA FITZGERALD**, singer
- ★ **CARTER FAMILY SINGERS**, recorded more than 300 mountain, folk, and country music songs
- ★ **WARREN BEATTY**, actor and director
- ★ **FREEMAN FISHER GOSDEN**, Amos of "Amos and Andy" radio show
- ★ **SHIRLEY MACLAINE**, actress
- ★ **MR. BOJANGLES** (Bill Robinson), dancer
- ★ **KATE SMITH**, famous for singing "God Bless America"
- ★ **GEORGE C. SCOTT**, actor
- ★ **WAYNE NEWTON**, singer and entertainer
- ★ **PATSY CLINE**, country singer

RIDDLE: Which person on the list above sang "Won't You Come Home, Bill Bailey?"

Answer: Pearl Bailey

Authors

Virginians' Pens Are Mightier than Swords!

- ANNE BEATTIE, stories and novels
- ANNIE DILLARD, WILLA CATHER, and ELLEN GLASGOW, Pulitzer Prize winners
  - JAMES BRANCH CABELL, romance novelist!
  - DOUGLAS SOUTHALL FREEMAN, biographer of Robert E. Lee and George Washington
  - EARL HAMNER, JR., creator of "The Waltons" TV show
  - EDGAR ALLAN POE, poet, short-story writer
- THOMAS KENNERLY WOLFE, Jr. novelist; known also for always wearing a white suit!
- CARTER GODWIN WOODSON, author of books on black culture
  - WILLARD HUNTINGTON WRIGHT (pen name, S.S. VanDine)—detective stories
  - LEE SMITH, novelist

Virginia Authors

Edgar Allan Poe was the creator of the modern detective story and the world's first fictional detective, C. Auguste Dupin.

nom de plume: French for pen name, a fictitious name a writer chooses to write under

RIDDLE: What famous Poe character was quoted as saying, "Nevermore"?

Answer: The Raven

Artists & More!

ARTISTS

MOSES JACOB EZEKIEL, sculptor, created the monument to Confederate dead in Arlington National Cemetery

EDWARD VIRGINIUS VALENTINE, sculptor of Thomas Jefferson and Stonewall Jackson

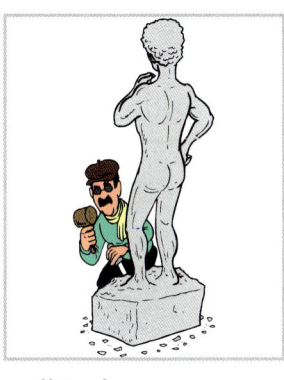

INVENTORS

CYRUS MCCORMICK, invented a reaping machine which revolutionized agriculture; founder, International Harvester Company

JOURNALISTS

VIRGINIUS DABNEY, editor, *Richmond Times-Dispatch*

ALF JOHNSON MAPP, JR., editorial writer, *The Virginia Pilot*

Educators - Scientists

EDUCATORS/TEACHERS

WILLIAM HOLMES MCGUFFEY, created a series of readers used in American schools for years—ask Grandma!

BOOKER T. WASHINGTON, a former slave whose influence on the education of blacks was enormous

EDMUND RUFFIN, founded the public education system in Virginia

SAMUEL CHAPMAN ARMSTRONG, founder of Hampton Normal & Industrial Institute

Educators and Scientists

DOCTORS AND SCIENTISTS

KATHERINE JOHNSON, NASA scientist and mathematician on the 1969 Apollo moon mission

SARAH GARLAND JONES, with her husband co-founded Richmond Community Hospital

WALTER REED, discovered that typhoid and yellow fever were spread by mosquito bites

Military Figures

SAILORS

MONITOR AND MERRIMAC, participated in the first battle of ironclad ships in 1862 at Hampton Roads

JOHN PAUL JONES, said "I have not yet begun to fight" when ordered to surrender during the Revolutionary War

MATTHEW FONTAINE MAURY, circumnavigated the globe 1826-1830

SOLDIERS

GEORGE ROGERS CLARK, Revolutionary War

THOMAS JONATHAN "STONEWALL" JACKSON, Civil War

"LIGHTHORSE HARRY" LEE, wrote that George Washington was "First in war, first in peace, and first in the hearts of his countrymen."

ROBERT E. LEE, commander of the Confederate Army

GEORGE MARSHALL, creator of the Marshall Plan which outlined the rebuilding of Europe after World War II

J.E.B. STUART, Confederate Army

General Jackson got his nickname "Stonewall" when he stood his ground during the First Battle of Bull Run (Manassas)

Patriots and Heroes

You Gotta Fight... For Your Right!

PATRIOTS
- Carter Braxton, Revolutionary War
- Patrick "Give Me Liberty or Give Me Death!" Henry, Revolutionary War
- John Paul "I have not yet begun to fight!" Jones, Revolutionary War
- Francis Lightfoot Lee, Virginia House of Burgesses
- Richard Henry Lee, signer, Declaration of Independence

HEROES
- Winfield Scott, hero, War of 1812

Word Definition

PATRIOT: one who loves, supports, and defends one's country

WAR OF 1812: conflict between the United States and Great Britain from 1812-1815, fought over neutral rights

Virginia Governors/Jurists

- Patrick Henry, first Virginia governor, 1776-79; 1784-86
- Thomas Jefferson, 1779-81
- Benjamin Harrison, 1781-84
- Edmund Jennings Randolph, 1786-88
- James Monroe, 1799-1802, 1811
- Peyton Randolph, 1811-12
- John Tyler, 1825-27
- Harry Flood Byrd, Sr., 1926-30
- L. Douglas Wilder, 1990-94

L. Douglas Wilder was the first African-American governor in the U.S., elected in 1989.

Virginia Governors/Jurists

JURISTS
- John Blair, Associate Justice, U.S. Supreme Court
- John Marshall, Chief Justice, U.S. Supreme Court
- Lewis Powell, Associate Justice, U.S. Supreme Court
- Edmund Jennings Randolph, U.S. Attorney General
- George Wythe, wrote the original Virginia protest against the Stamp Act; first professor of law in the U.S., at the College of William and Mary

Churches and Schools

Keeping the Faith

Bruton Parish Church, Williamsburg—Governors, councillors, and other officials of colonial Virginia worshiped here.

Lee Chapel, Lexington—Burial place of Robert E. Lee housing statue of Lee by Virginia-born sculptor, Edward Virginius Valentine.

St. John's Church, Richmond—It was here that Patrick Henry made his "Give me liberty or give me death!" speech.

SCHOOLS

Some of Virginia's colleges and universities:

- University of Virginia, Charlottesville; founded by Thomas Jefferson
- Virginia Polytechnic Institute, Blacksburg
- Virginia Commonwealth University, Richmond
- Old Dominion University, Norfolk
- George Mason University, Fairfax
- College of William and Mary, Williamsburg
- Washington and Lee University, Lexington
- Virginia Military Institute, Lexington
- James Madison University, Harrisonburg

Churches and Schools

The first free schools in the U.S. were established in Virginia!

Historic Sites and Parks

Historic Sites
★ Appomattox Court House
★ Jamestown
★ Colonial Williamsburg
★ Arlington National Cemetery

Parks
★ Breaks Interstate Park, Virginia/Kentucky border, on the rim of the largest river canyon east of the Mississippi River!

★ Clinch Mountain State Park, Russell County, largest state park in Virginia

★ Colonial National Historical Park, Yorktown

★ Harpers Ferry National Historical Park covers land in Virginia, West Virginia, and Maryland!

★ Jamestown Festival Park—site of the first English settlement in the New World

★ Shenandoah National Park, near Luray

Historic Sites and Parks

67

Home, Sweet Home!

Early Residency

★ Ash Lawn-Highland, home of President James Monroe

★ Bacon's Castle on the James River

★ Berkeley Plantation, Charles City

★ Carter's Grove Plantation, Williamsburg

★ Gunston Hall, on the Potomac River, home of George Mason

★ Monticello, Charlottesville, home of Thomas Jefferson

★ Montpelier, near Orange, home of James Madison

Home, Sweet Home

★ Mount Vernon, near Alexandria, home of George and Martha Washington

★ Shirley Plantation, on the James River

★ Stonewall Jackson House, Lexington

★ Stratford Hall, ancestral home of Robert E. Lee

★ White House of the Confederacy, Richmond

Battlefields

A few of Virginia's famous BATTLEFIELDS

- Appomattox Court House National Historical Park
- Ball's Bluff, Fairfax
- Cedar Creek and Belle Grove, Middletown
- Chancellorsville Battlefield
- Fredericksburg and Spotsylvania National Military Park
- Manassas National Battlefield Park
- New Market Battlefield Park
- Petersburg National Battlefield
- Richmond National Battlefield Park 
- Sailors Creek, Green Bay
- The Wilderness Battlefield
- Yorktown

Battlefields

Richmond was the capital of the Confederate States of America for most of the Civil War.

Virginia boasted a record 91 Confederate generals!

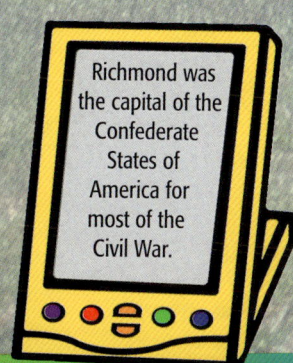

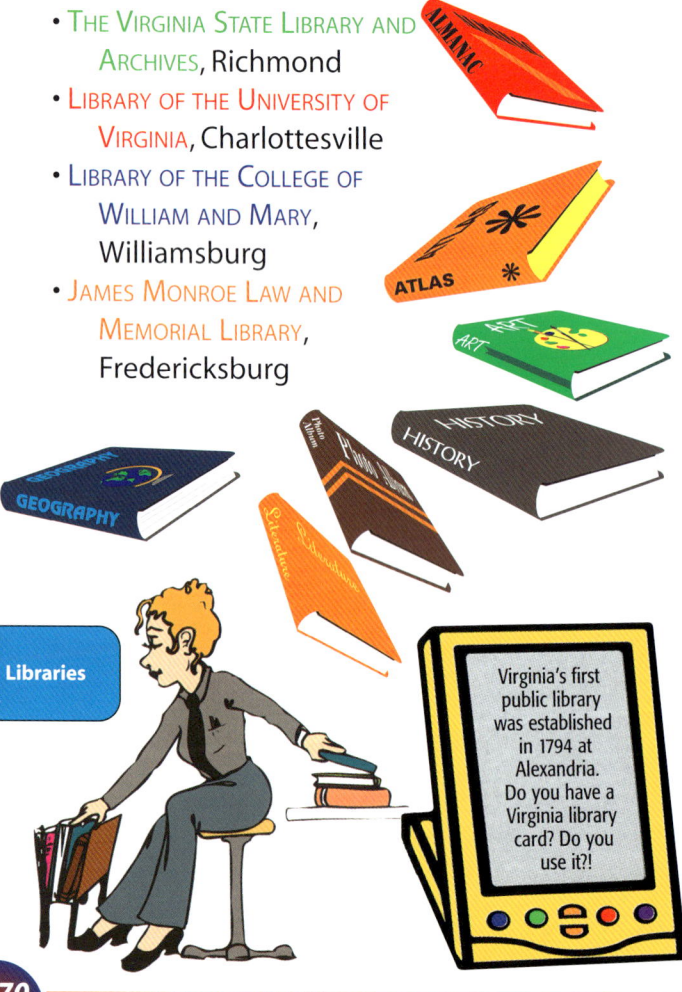

Libraries

- THE VIRGINIA STATE LIBRARY AND ARCHIVES, Richmond
- LIBRARY OF THE UNIVERSITY OF VIRGINIA, Charlottesville
- LIBRARY OF THE COLLEGE OF WILLIAM AND MARY, Williamsburg
- JAMES MONROE LAW AND MEMORIAL LIBRARY, Fredericksburg

Libraries

Virginia's first public library was established in 1794 at Alexandria. Do you have a Virginia library card? Do you use it?!

Zoos & Animal Parks

BLUEBIRD GAP FARM, Hampton
CHINCOTEAGUE NATIONAL WILDLIFE REFUGE
DINOSAUR LAND, White Post
EASTERN SHORE OF VIRGINIA NATIONAL WILDLIFE REFUGE
INSECT ZOO, Woodbridge
LURAY REPTILE CENTER AND DINOSAUR PARK
MILL MOUNTAIN ZOOLOGICAL PARK, Roanoke
ON THE WILD SIDE ZOOLOGICAL PARK, Madison
RESTON ANIMAL PARK, Vienna
VIRGINIA HIGHLAND LLAMAS, Bland
VIRGINIA LIVING MUSEUM, Newport News
VIRGINIA MARINE SCIENCE MUSEUM, Virginia Beach
VIRGINIA ZOOLOGICAL PARK, Norfolk

Zoos & Animal Parks

Museums

- VIRGINIA MUSEUM OF FINE ARTS, Richmond
- SCIENCE MUSEUM OF VIRGINIA, Richmond
- CHRYSLER MUSEUM, Norfolk
- MARINERS' MUSEUM, Newport News
- EDGAR ALLAN POE MUSEUM, Richmond
  - MUSEUM OF AMERICAN FRONTIER CULTURE, Staunton
  - MUSEUM OF THE CONFEDERACY, Richmond
  - VIRGINIA TRANSPORTATION MUSEUM, Roanoke
  - WAR MEMORIAL MUSEUM OF VIRGINIA, Newport News
  - NEWSEUM, Arlington
- ALEXANDRIA ARCHAEOLOGY MUSEUM
- HAMPTON ROADS NAVAL MUSEUM
- VIRGINIA DISCOVERY MUSEUM, Charlottesville
- RICHMOND CHILDRENS' MUSEUM

Museums

Monuments & Places

MONUMENTS

BOOKER T. WASHINGTON NATIONAL MONUMENT, near Burnt Chimney

GEORGE WASHINGTON BIRTHPLACE NATIONAL MONUMENT, Westmoreland County

TOMB OF THE UNKNOWNS, Arlington National Cemetery

SPACE PLACE!

NASA Langley Visitor/Research Center, Hampton. See a Moon rock, the Apollo Command Module, and a space suit worn on the Moon!

Monuments and Places

The Arts

WOLF TRAP FARM PARK FOR THE PERFORMING ARTS, Vienna

THE BARTER THEATRE, Abingdon (It was founded during the Great Depression in the 1930s. It got its name when farmers bartered crops for tickets!)

SHAKESPEARE FESTIVAL, Williamsburg

THE LONG WAY HOME —a play about a heroic pioneer woman who survived a 1756 Indian attack!

TRAIL OF THE LONESOME PINE — The story of Virginia coal mining

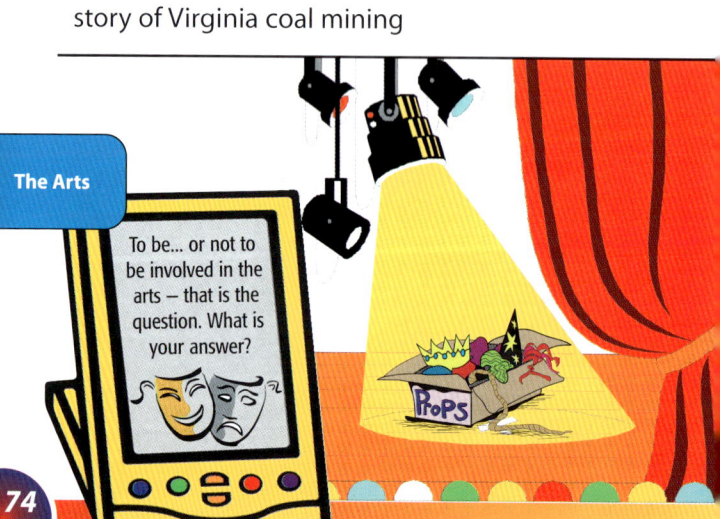

The Arts

To be... or not to be involved in the arts — that is the question. What is your answer?

Seashores & Lighthouses

SEASHORES
Assateague Island National Seashore, home of the wild ponies!

LIGHTHOUSES
The candy-cane colored Assateague Lighthouse has warned mariners away from the treacherous shoals since 1833!

Seashores & Lighthouses

75

Roads, Bridges & More!

ROADS

BLUE RIDGE PARKWAY, the longest scenic drive in the world!

SKYLINE DRIVE, in Shenandoah National Park, runs through the Blue Ridge Mountains

BRIDGES, TUNNELS AND CHIMNEYS

CHESAPEAKE BAY BRIDGE-TUNNEL — 23 miles (37 km) long, it links the Virginia Beach/Norfolk area with Virginia's Eastern Shore

NATURAL BRIDGE OF VIRGINIA, 215 feet (66 meters) high; a highway runs across this natural wonder!

NATURAL CHIMNEYS, near Mt. Solon. Seven limestone towers rise 120 feet (37 meters)

NATURAL TUNNEL, near Gate City, was cut through a mountain by a creek; 850 feet (260 m) long and 100 feet (30 m) high.

Roads, Bridges & More!

Swamps and Caverns

SWAMPS

THE GREAT DISMAL SWAMP NATIONAL WILDLIFE REFUGE, on the Virginia/North Carolina border near Suffolk. The swamp was surveyed in 1763 by George Washington.

CAVERNS

- LURAY CAVERNS
- SHENANDOAH CAVERNS, a rainbow of rock!
- SKYLINE CAVERNS, near Front Royal, has rare, flowerlike rock formations of calcite

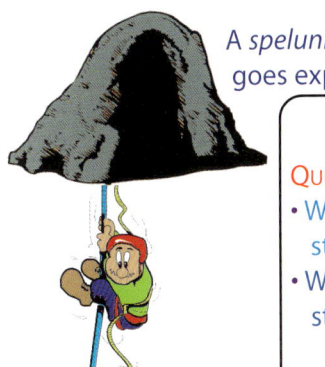

A *spelunker* is a person who goes exploring caves!

QUESTION:
- Which is the stalagmite?
- Which is the stalactite?

Swamps and Caverns

ANSWER: Stalactites are long, tapering formations hanging from the roof of a cavern, produced by continuous watery deposits containing certain minerals. The mineral-rich water dripping from stalactites often forms conical stalagmites on the floor below.

Animals

Animals of Virginia

Virginia animals include:

- White-tailed Deer
- Black Bear
- Bobcat
- Opossum
- Raccoon
- Fox 
- Elk
- Nutria
- Skunk
- Squirrel
- Rabbit
- Beaver
- Mink
- River Otter

Virginia Animals

The Virginia Opossum is North America's only marsupial (pouched mammal). An opossum may "play possum" and pretend it is dead to escape an enemy!

Wildlife Watch

GIDDY-UP!
- THE WILD PONIES OF CHINCOTEAGUE -

Virginia's wild ponies live on Chincoteague Island on the Eastern Shore. It is believed that they may have come ashore during the 16th century when a Spanish galleon shipwrecked. Each year the ponies are herded across the inlet to Assateague Island and the foals are auctioned off.

> "Misty" is the name of a famous wild pony. If you check your library, you can probably find a book to read about Misty!

Birds

You may spy these birds in Virginia:

Pileated Woodpecker
Prothonotary Warbler
Northern Oriole
Scarlet Tanager
Grosbeak
Hummingbird
Peewee
Swift
Wild Turkey
Woodcock
Ibis

Wood Duck

Quail

Wren

Mourning Dove

Tern

Thrush

Virginia Birds

A hummingbird's wings beat 75 times a second—so fast that you only see a blur! They make short, squeaky sounds, but do not sing.

Ruffed Grouse

Insects

Don't let these Virginia bugs bug you!

- Beetle
- Cicada
- Cricket
- Dragonfly
- Firefly
- Honeybee
- Katydid
- Mayfly
- Mosquito
- Moth
- Termite
- Walking Stick
- Weevil
- Yellow Jacket

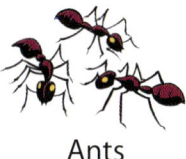

Bumblebee

Ants

Butterfly

Ladybug

Praying Mantis

Grasshopper

Do we know any of these bugs?

Maybe... Hey, that ladybug is cute!

Whirligig Beetles have two pairs of eyes — one pair looks above the water, the other under it!

Virginia Insects

Fish

SWIMMING IN VIRGINIA WATERS:

- Bass
- Bream
- Bluegill
- Carp
- Catfish
- Crappie
- Perch
- Sunfish
- Croaker
- Hogfish
- Menhaden
- Sea Bass
- Flounder
- Striped Bass
- Sea Trout

Virginia Fish

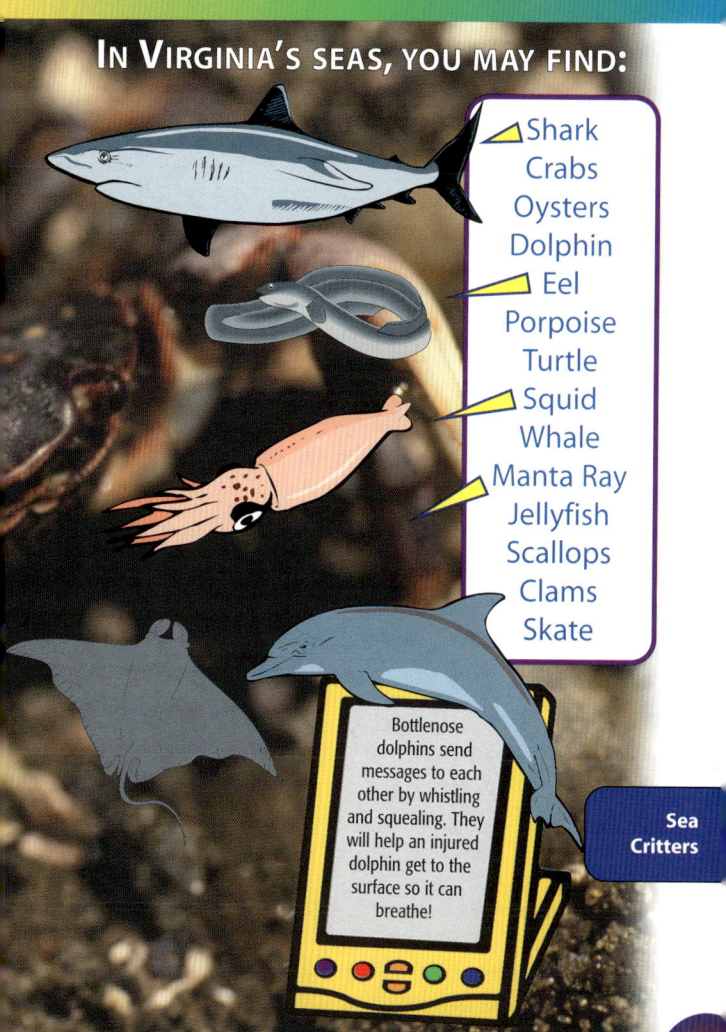

Sea Critters

IN VIRGINIA'S SEAS, YOU MAY FIND:

- Shark
- Crabs
- Oysters
- Dolphin
- Eel
- Porpoise
- Turtle
- Squid
- Whale
- Manta Ray
- Jellyfish
- Scallops
- Clams
- Skate

Bottlenose dolphins send messages to each other by whistling and squealing. They will help an injured dolphin get to the surface so it can breathe!

Sea Critters

83

Seashells

She sells seashells by the Virginia seashore!

Auger Shell

Cerith
Slipper Shell
Worm Shell
Helmet Shell
Wentletrap
Janthina
Whelk
Vampire Shell
Sundial Shell

Bubble Shell
Tusk Shell
Mussel
Oyster
Scallop
Cockle
Angel Wing
Shipworm

Olive Shell

Periwinkle

Moon Shell

Seashells

Prehistoric fossils of snails, shells, and corals 400 million years old are embedded in Virginia's capitol building's floors in Richmond!

Coquina

84

Trees

TREEMENDOUS!
THESE TREES TOWER OVER VIRGINIA:

- Black Tupelo
- Sweet Gum
- Poplar
- Locust
- Ash
- Oak
- Pine
- Birch

Virginia Trees

Wildflowers

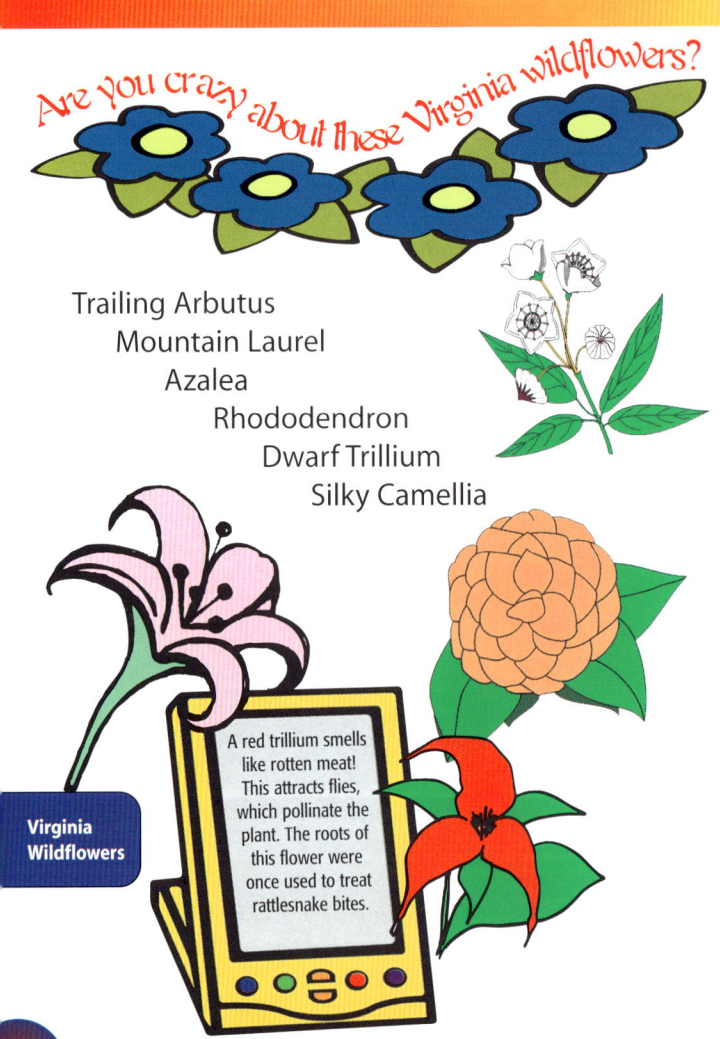

Are you crazy about these Virginia wildflowers?

Trailing Arbutus
  Mountain Laurel
    Azalea
      Rhododendron
        Dwarf Trillium
          Silky Camellia

Virginia Wildflowers

A red trillium smells like rotten meat! This attracts flies, which pollinate the plant. The roots of this flower were once used to treat rattlesnake bites.

Cream of the Crops

Virginia's principal agricultural products:

- Chickens
- Corn
- Milk
- Tobacco
- Hogs
- Yams (sweet potatoes)
- Peanuts
- Peaches
- Seafood
- Beef Cattle
- Soybeans
- Turkeys
- Wheat
- Apples
- Hay

Cream of the Crops

First/Big/Small/Etc.

1619 - First official Thanksgiving in America, Berkeley Plantation

1833 - First steam-driven railroad

1846 - Hollins College, Roanoke County, first college chartered for women

1862 - First battle of ironclad ships (Monitor and Merrimac), Hampton Roads

1915 - First human voice sent by radio from Arlington to Hawaii and France

1975 - Biggest ice cream sundae (777 gallons of ice cream!), McLean

GEORGE WASHINGTON: America's first president, engineer, realtor, cartographer, scientific farmer, stock breeder, military strategist and efficiency expert!

Festivals

APPLE BLOSSOM FESTIVAL, held in spring in Winchester.

GARDEN WEEK, held in April when hundreds of historic houses and gardens are opened to public.

JAMESTOWN LANDING DAY, held in May at Williamsburg to commemorate the founding of the first permanent English colony in America.

OYSTER FESTIVAL, held in October on Chincoteague Island.

WIZARDS, WITCHES AND WARLOCKS ON THE WATERFRONT, held on Halloween in Norfolk, is Hampton Roads' GRANDEST costume ball!

FOODS AND FEASTS IN 17TH CENTURY VIRGINIA, held on Thanksgiving weekend in Williamsburg, is devoted to the foods of the Jamestown colonists and their Powhatan neighbors.

Festivals

Holidays

Calendar

Lee-Jackson-King Days, *in January*	Presidents' Day, *3rd Monday in February*	Memorial Day, *last Monday in May*
Independence Day, July 4	Columbus Day, *2nd Monday in October*	Veteran's Day, November 11

Notes: _____

Thanksgiving: The first one was celebrated at Berkeley Plantation in 1619.

Holidays

Famous Food

Virginia is famous for the following delicious foods!

- Apples
- Succotash
- Marmalade
- Shoofly Pie
- Spoon Bread
- Hoppin' John
- Apoquinimine Cakes
- Corn Pone
- Seafood Chowder
- Red-eye Gravy
- Apple Cider
- Smoked Ham
- Beaten Biscuits

Ye Olde Williamsburg Colonial Tavern Menu

~Side Items & Bread~

- Cauliflower Pickles
- Pickled Oysters
- Spoon Bread: a baked dish made of cornmeal, eggs, and shortenin' (butter or lard – in other words, fat!)
- Shortenin' Bread: crispy & flaky
- Corn Pone: a loaf or oval-shaped bread or cake. This one's got corn in it.
- Hand-churned Butter
- Peach Marmalade: jelly or preserves with small pieces of fruit or rind in it.

~Soup & Salad~

- Parsnip or Clam Chowder: A thick, creamy soup, made with clams, vegetables, or whatever we can get.
- Peanut Soup
- Oyster Soup
- Stewed Cabbage with Ham Hock (a pig's ankle – yummy!)
- "Salat" (Salad) Greens with Turnips

~Drinks~

- Sassafras Bark Tea: Sassafras is a tree that grows in these parts. We use the leaves, bark, and oil from the roots for flavor.
- Apple Cider
- Hot Cranberry Punch

~Dinners~

- Deviled Crab Cakes: we make 'em spicy with lots of hot seasonings!
- Smoked Ham & Red-eye Gravy (pan gravy made from fried ham)
- Pork in Apple Cider
- Chicken Smothered in Oysters
- Roast Long Potatoes
- Winter Squash
- Sweet Potato Pone
- Hoppin' John: a true Southern dish made with black-eyed peas, rice, and salt pork or bacon
- Succotash: a dish made of corn and beans (usually lima beans, but we'll use anything!)

~Desserts~

- Raspberry Fool: an English dessert made of crushed, cooked fruit mixed with cream or custard and served cold
- Plum Pudding with Hard Sauce (a topping made from creamed butter and confectioner's (powdered) sugar)
- Wet Bottom Shoofly Pie: a pie filled with a mixture of flour, butter, brown sugar, and molasses. We don't put a crust on top.
- Burnt Sugar Cake: it's only slightly burnt!
- Indian Pudding: cornmeal mush sweetened with molasses. Sometimes dressed up with sugar, eggs, raisins, and spices.
- Molasses Fruitcake: as if it wasn't sticky enough, we put more molasses in!
- Ginger Cakes
- Apple Custard

Famous Food

91

Business & Trade

Virginia enjoys an active business trade in the retail and wholesale marketplace. The state imports many goods, such as oil, and exports many goods, primarily coal.

Virginia's chief industries are services, government, manufacturing, tourism, and agriculture.

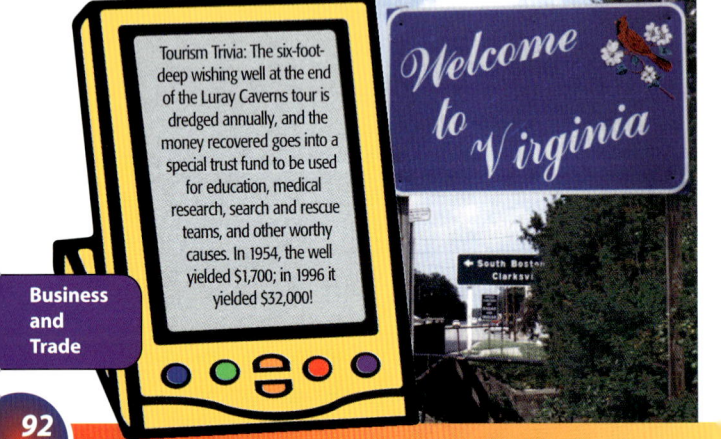

Tourism Trivia: The six-foot-deep wishing well at the end of the Luray Caverns tour is dredged annually, and the money recovered goes into a special trust fund to be used for education, medical research, search and rescue teams, and other worthy causes. In 1954, the well yielded $1,700; in 1996 it yielded $32,000!

Business and Trade

Virginia Books & Websites

My First Book About Virginia by Carole Marsh
America the Beautiful: Virginia by Sylvia McNair
From Sea to Shining Sea: Virginia by Dennis Fradin
Hello USA: Virginia by Karen Sirvaitis
Let's Discover the States: Virginia by the Aylesworths
Portrait of America: Virginia by Kathleen Thompson
The Virginia Experience by Carole Marsh

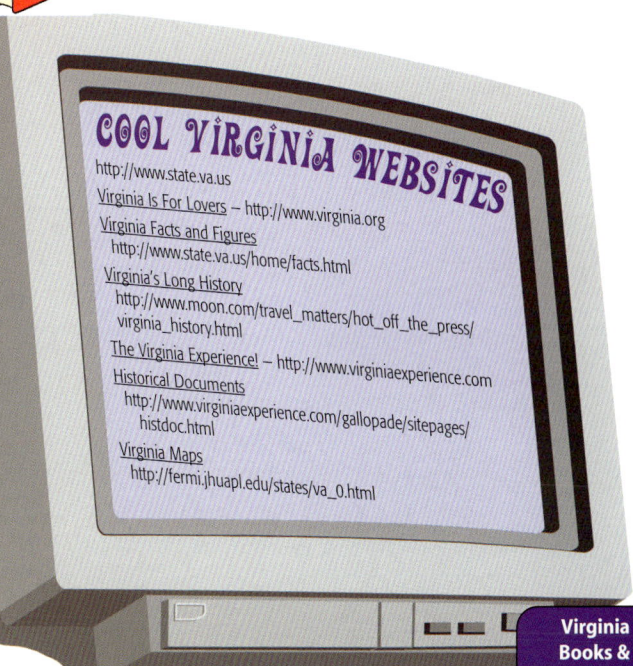

Cool Virginia Websites

http://www.state.va.us

Virginia Is For Lovers – http://www.virginia.org

Virginia Facts and Figures
http://www.state.va.us/home/facts.html

Virginia's Long History
http://www.moon.com/travel_matters/hot_off_the_press/virginia_history.html

The Virginia Experience! – http://www.virginiaexperience.com

Historical Documents
http://www.virginiaexperience.com/gallopade/sitepages/histdoc.html

Virginia Maps
http://fermi.jhuapl.edu/states/va_0.html

Glossary

Glossary Words

abolitionist: a person opposed to slavery
burgess: a representative of the people
colony: a region controlled by a distant country
commonwealth: for the good of the people
constitution: a document outlining the role of a government
dominion: a self-governed body
emancipation: to be set free
federalist: in favor of a strong central government
immigrant: a person who comes to a new country to live
indentured: to work for someone for a set period of time in exchange for something
manumission: to be freed from slavery
pentagon: something with five sides
revolution: the overthrow of a government
secede: to voluntarily give up being a part of an organized group

Spelling List

inia Spelling Bee

Here are some special Virginia-related words to learn! To take the Spelling Bee, have someone call out the words and you spell them aloud or write them on a piece of paper.

Spelling Words

Appalachian	Manassas
Berkeley	Norfolk
Braxton	Occoquan
Chickahominy	Potomac
Delmarva	Quilting Bee
Emporia	Roanoke
Fredericksburg	Shenandoah
Galax	Tidewater
Harpers Ferry	University of Virginia
Iron Gate	Vienna
Jefferson	Wahunsonacock
Kilmarnock	Yorktown
Luray	

Spelling List

About the Author

ABOUT THE AUTHOR...

CAROLE MARSH has been writing about Virginia for more than 20 years. She is the author of the popular Virginia State Stuff series for young readers and creator, along with her son, Michael Marsh, of "Virginia Facts and Factivities," a CD-ROM widely used in Virginia schools. The Byrd side of her family history led the author to spend a great deal of time researching, writing, and making photographs in Virginia. The author of more than 100 Virginia books and other supplementary educational materials, Marsh is currently working on a new collection of Virginia materials for young people. Marsh correlates her Virginia materials to Virginia's Standards of Learning. Many of her books and other materials have been inspired by or requested by Virginia teachers and librarians.